The Eighth Name

by Belinda Chavremootoo

Dedication

For those who were told to forget.

And for those who remembered anyway.

Text Copyright

About the Author

Belinda writes charming cozy mysteries filled with seaside secrets, garden gates, and cats who always know the truth. When not plotting fictional crimes, she can be found in her own garden where the earthy scent of soil and the gentle rustle of leaves provide inspiration. Her two cats supervising everything with quiet judgment.

Explore more at her Amazon Author Page:

https://www.amazon.ca/stores/author/B0DKC4VZ5K/allbooks

Table of Contents

Prologue

She was already dead when the tide reached her.

The sea lapped gently against the rocks beneath the Whispering Cliffs, not yet storming, not yet wild. It was the kind of stillness that only came before the breaking.

A shell lay nestled between the woman's lips—smooth, polished, deliberate. Her fingers clutched a half-wet notebook. Her eyes were open.

Far above, the final ferry vanished over the horizon.

And in a quiet house on the edge of the island, a satchel waited.

Inside were the names of seven families.

And a space where an eighth should have been.

The island had forgotten.

But the sea had not.

Chapter 1

The sea hissed against the dock like a warning, restless under the bruised sky. Clouds gathered low, thick as wet wool, and the wind carried the scent of salt and something older—like wood smoke and rusted secrets. Somewhere in the distance, a bell clanged once, long and hollow.

Detective Naila Deshmukh stood at the edge of the stone jetty; her boots planted wide against the spray-slick moss. She had been on the island of Varuka for six months, and it still felt like standing on a lid someone was trying to keep shut.

Varuka was a crescent-shaped island, the largest in a forgotten chain between Madagascar and Sri Lanka. It had no airport, only a once-weekly ferry. Its people clung to old ways: stories passed through generations, laws written in salt and silence. Every cove had a secret, every house an altar. Tourists called it "untouched." Naila called it guarded.

She had grown up hearing her grandmother's stories about Varuka—the myths, the songs, the warnings. But they'd been bedtime tales, not blueprints. Her own parents had left the island before she was born, and she'd only returned now because of a fall from grace in her Interpol career. A dead informant. A case that went wrong. A scapegoat was needed—and she was too principled for politics.

Here, she wore the uniform of Police Chief, but she might as well have been wearing a mask. Most locals barely spoke to her. The ones who did, did so with careful neutrality, like handling a knife by the blade.

The ferry groaned as it pulled in, its hull mottled with rust. Waves slapped against the pilings, eager to swallow something. This was the last crossing before the monsoon began—six weeks of rain, wind, and isolation. The sea would close its doors like a prison gate.

She watched passengers disembark: locals hauling burlap sacks, children clutching tins of condensed milk, and two unlucky tourists who clearly hadn't read the travel advisories. The tourists were met by a silent driver from the south village and quickly hustled into a van with fogged windows.

Then came Captain Haru Setele, the ferry master and self-appointed gatekeeper of the island.

"You're cutting it close," Naila said as he came down the ramp.

He gave her a dry smile. "We always do. You just never noticed before."

He looked older than he had last month—maybe the sea aged him faster. Or maybe the island did that to people who knew too much.

"Manifest clean?" she asked.

"Groceries. Petrol drums. Two crates of school books. That's all."

"And the passengers?"

He hesitated. "Count matches the log."

It didn't. Naila was sure of it. One woman—slim, in a long linen coat and oversized sunglasses—had slipped off the ferry without so much as a glance. Her face was hidden, but her posture... there was something studied about it. Too careful.

Before Naila could move to follow, the woman vanished into the tangled alleyways near the fish market. The kind of alleys where eyes watched from behind curtains and everyone knew everyone—and no one knew anything.

She started after her.

Then came the shout.

"Chief! You need to see this!"

Constable Arem—young, nervous, eager to please—was waving wildly from the trailhead by the Whispering Cliffs. The cliffs rose above the western shore like broken teeth, white with bird droppings and legends. Locals claimed they echoed back words you never said aloud.

Naila jogged across the cracked stone path, her breath tight in her chest. She passed fishing nets hung like ghosts to dry, prayer flags fluttering with wet wishes, and children with bare feet and suspicious eyes.

Arem led her down a goat trail slick with moss. The tide was high, gnawing at the rocks below. At the bottom lay a woman's body—twisted, still, clothes soaked to the waist. Her white hair clung to her face like seaweed.

The body lay twisted on the rocks, half-soaked by the tide. Pale. Still.

Naila knelt beside the corpse. It took her a moment to reconcile the lifeless face with the vivid woman she remembered.

Dr. Rhea Kaoro had been sixty-eight, though she moved and argued like someone twenty years younger. She had lived alone in a crumbling stone house near the cliffs, surrounded by books, string-bound scrolls, and jars filled with salt-worn relics. Her daughter, Miri, was an artist living abroad—last Naila had heard, she was in Nairobi or maybe Paris. They hadn't spoken in years. Not after the funeral of Rhea's husband, a marine biologist who drowned under strange circumstances when Miri was still a teenager.

Rhea had never remarried. She had said once, in a rare moment of candour, *"Myths are more loyal than men. And more honest."*

Her hair, usually pulled into a tight knot with carved bone pins, was now loose and wild with seaweed. Her weathered skin, always browned by sun and sea air, looked oddly pale in death. She was dressed in a faded indigo wrap—homespun, traditional—and around her neck hung her usual string of coral beads.

Naila gently pried open the dead woman's mouth.

Inside, nestled behind her teeth, was a small cowrie shell—polished, white, and wrong.

Arem muttered something under his breath. A prayer, maybe.

"Did she fall?" he asked.

Naila shook her head slowly. "Maybe."

But everything about the scene felt arranged. The shell. The calm expression. The missing satchel Rhea was never without.

She stood, the wind lifting strands of her hair like sea thread. "Someone wanted this to look like an accident."

Arem swallowed. "But why?"

Naila looked back up at the cliffs, her voice quiet.

"Because Rhea Kaoro knew too many stories. And some people on this island would kill to keep theirs buried."

And somewhere behind her, back in the alleyways or deep in the cliffs, the killer was already listening.

Chapter 2

By dawn, the tide had receded, but the questions had only grown.

Naila stood alone in the makeshift morgue—an old storeroom converted with little more than a steel table and overhead fan that ticked out the seconds like a metronome. Outside, the storm clouds hadn't broken, but the air was thick with waiting. The monsoon hovered just offshore, patient and hungry.

Rhea Kaoro's body lay covered in a white cotton sheet. The shell was sealed in an evidence bag resting beside it. Naila held it to the light again: a cowrie, smooth, old, the kind once used for currency or ritual offerings. A symbol of protection—or warning, depending on which version of the legend you believed.

And this was Varuka, where every symbol had five meanings and none of them safe.

"Time of death?" she asked without looking up.

Constable Arem, still pale from the night's discovery, checked his notes. "Local doctor estimates late evening. Maybe between nine and midnight. No signs of external trauma."

"Except for being dead on the rocks."

He nodded, hesitating. "There's… no sign she fell from the top. No disturbed gravel. No dragging. Her sandals were still on. Too tidy, isn't it?"

Naila grunted. "Someone placed her there. Quietly."

He shifted. "Do you think it's—uh—the Whisperers?"

The word hung in the air like smoke.

"Don't start," Naila muttered. "We're not dealing in ghost stories."

But part of her wasn't sure.

*****

Later that morning, Naila walked to Rhea Kaoro's house—a squat stone cottage on a hill just outside the old village. It had been standing for over a century, built during the colonial period when scholars came to "collect" Varuka's culture like butterflies in glass boxes.

Rhea had taken it back in her own way. Books spilled from every surface—many in Varukan, some handwritten. The air smelled like dried herbs and candle wax. A kettle still sat cold on the stove; a tin of sea tea open beside it.

There were no signs of forced entry.

No spilled drawers. No broken locks.

But the satchel—the one Rhea always carried—was missing.

It had been leather, old and soft, filled with notes and translations, sometimes leaves or shells pressed between pages. If Rhea had made a discovery worth killing for, it would have been in that bag.

She found something else, though.

On the writing desk, tucked under an open book, was a torn scrap of paper. A single line written in shaky ink:

"The truth is older than the island."

Naila stared at it for a long time.

***

Back at the station, Arem returned with the ferry passenger log.

"There was no woman in a coat listed," he said. "Manifest doesn't mention anyone matching her description."

"She was hiding something," Naila said. "Or someone's hiding her."

She tapped the shell again, sealed in plastic. "Find out where this type of cowrie is usually found. If it's local or imported."

Arem nodded, then hesitated. "Do we contact the daughter?"

Naila sighed. "Yes. Contact Miri Kaoro. I'll speak with her when she arrives."

"You think she'll come?"

"I think she'll come angry."

***

Meanwhile, far from Varuka, in a cramped studio apartment in Nairobi, a phone buzzed against a cluttered table of brushes, receipts, and dried paint tubes. A call from a number Miri hadn't seen in years. The island.

She stared at it, already knowing before she answered.

Some stories begin with a death.

Others only wake up when one happens.

***

The clinic smelled like menthol and mould—an old colonial structure turned health post, its whitewashed walls streaked by years of salt wind and rust. A ceiling fan turned above Naila's head, moving the heavy air without cooling it.

Dr. Enzo Malraux stood at the sink, washing his hands like he couldn't get them clean enough. He was lean, sun-weathered, and carried himself like a man used to being left alone. His tie was crooked. His glasses fogged slightly in the humid air.

"You're not here for a checkup," he said, drying his hands on a linen towel.

"You did the prelim on Rhea Kaoro," Naila said.

He turned, slowly. "I examined her, yes. She had no visible injuries. No signs of assault. No defensive wounds. No broken bones."

"She was placed," Naila said. "You saw it. You know it."

He didn't answer immediately. He crossed to the tiny refrigerator and pulled out a bottle of water, offering her one. She declined.

"I know Rhea," he said. "Knew her. We grew up on the same ridge, went to the same school before she left for the university in France. She was proud. Independent. She walked the cliffs often. Maybe she slipped."

"She had a shell in her mouth."

Now he looked at her.

"The shell. Did you mention it to the Elders?"

"I'm not asking their permission to investigate a death."

"You don't need their permission," he said. "But you'll get their attention. And that's not always healthy on this island."

Naila crossed her arms. "So, you'll just write this off as natural causes?"

"I didn't say that." He took off his glasses and wiped them. "But without access to labs or a coroner's office, I can't make a formal ruling of homicide. There's no blunt force trauma, no indication of poison—at least not one I can detect here. If you want an autopsy, you'll have to wait until the sea calms and someone from the mainland can come. That's six weeks minimum. If they agree to it at all."

Naila's jaw tightened. "You're saying I have to build a murder case without a body I can prove was murdered."

"I'm saying this isn't Interpol. You don't have a lab. You don't have a forensics team. You have guesses, instincts, and local politics. Be careful which one you rely on first."

They stared at each other for a long moment. Then Malraux added quietly:

"Let her daughter bury her in peace, Naila. You stir this, the island will remember."

She turned to go.

"I don't care if the island remembers," she said. "I care that someone thinks they can kill a woman for knowing too much—and get away with it."

Chapter 3

The island rose from the sea like a memory Miri Kaoro had tried to drown.

Through the ferry's salt-streaked window, Varuka looked smaller than she remembered—just a crescent of jungle and cliffs under a low, churning sky. But the moment the boat drew close enough for her to smell the humid mix of brine, wet stone, and cooking fires, the ache in her chest returned, sharp and specific.

Grief wore many faces. On Miri, it wore irritation and a sore jaw from clenching her teeth since Nairobi.

She hadn't seen her mother in over five years. Their last phone call had ended in silence, not shouting—but the kind of silence that hardened into walls.

Still, when the island police had called and said *there's been a death*, she'd known before they said the name.

Rhea Kaoro was dead.

Now Miri was coming home, whether she liked it or not.

***

At the dock, Detective Naila Deshmukh waited in a clean, pressed uniform, her posture impossibly straight. Miri remembered her vaguely—once a name in her mother's conversations. The "mainland policewoman with island blood."

"You came," Naila said.

"I'm not here to swap recipes," Miri replied, stepping off the boat with a leather duffel slung across one shoulder. "Where is she?"

"She's been moved to the clinic morgue. I can take you there. But first… we need to talk."

Miri stopped walking. "Talk? Or brief me?"

"I'd rather tell you everything in private."

There was a pause. Miri studied the detective— the crisp edges, the polite distance, the guarded eyes.

Everything on this island had to be wrapped in ritual. Even grief.

"Fine," Miri said. "Talk fast."

***

They sat in the station's side office. The windows rattled slightly with the pressure of the coming storm.

"She didn't fall," Naila said. "That's what you're about to ask me. The official record might not say murder. But I will."

Miri's hands tightened around the ceramic mug she hadn't touched.

"Do you have proof?"

"There was a shell in her mouth," Naila said. "A polished cowrie. Placed there. There were no injuries. No signs of a fall. No robbery. No bag. Whoever did this wanted it to look natural."

Miri blinked slowly. "You think she was… killed because of her research?"

"I think your mother found something someone didn't want rediscovered."

Miri let the words sit for a moment, her expression unreadable.

Then she laughed. It was short and dry. "Of course she did. She couldn't help herself. Even when no one was listening."

"She was working on something new?"

"She never stopped. She was obsessed with an old oral legend that the Council banned from formal teaching years ago—something about the 'lost salt families.' Said the official history was a lie."

"Did she ever mention the *Sea Whisperers?*"

Miri flinched at the name. "She said they weren't myth. Just forgotten people who remembered how to stay hidden."

Naila leaned forward. "I think your mother died for remembering."

***

Later, as the rain finally broke and thunder echoed over the cliffs, Miri stood outside the morgue.

She hadn't yet gone in.

In her hand was the old leather satchel her mother used to carry—battered, dusty, smelling like incense and old parchment. Naila had recovered it that morning from the southern beach, where a fisherman had found it buried in sand and wrapped in oilcloth.

Inside were notebooks. Water-damaged. Torn.

But one page was dry and intact.

A map. Drawn in ink. Of Varuka's western cliffs—and a location marked only by a circle and a word in old Varukan script.

Miri traced the word with her finger.

"Buried."

Chapter 4

Miri hadn't cried yet.

Not on the ferry. Not in the morgue. Not even when she touched the cold skin of her mother's hand, as if expecting some last message to rise up through the silence.

Instead, she sat alone in the back room of her mother's house—what had once been her childhood bedroom. The paint on the walls had faded to dust-coloured streaks, and the carved wooden bed felt smaller than it used to. A single framed photo still hung above it: Miri at ten, half-smiling, hair in a messy braid, one arm slung around her father, the other around Rhea. All three of them squinting in the island sun.

The glass was cracked.

She leaned her head back and closed her eyes.

***

There had been so many arguments.

Her mother wanted her to stay, to *inherit* something Miri didn't understand. The stories. The language. The soil. But Miri had wanted colour, movement, noise—she wanted Nairobi, Paris, the messy, kinetic chaos of the mainland. She wanted to paint in warehouses and fall in love with people who believed in possibility instead of prophecy.

When her father drowned, everything hardened. Rhea withdrew into her research, and Miri withdrew into distance. First emotionally, then literally. Her mother never begged her to stay. She just stopped asking her to come back.

The worst part was, they hadn't fought when Miri left. They'd just… stopped talking.

***

She rose from the bed and wandered into the study. Papers were stacked like altars. Books marked with feathers and shells. One notebook lay open, pages warped by moisture. Her mother's handwriting was still sharp, still deliberate.

"They say the salt families vanished. But they were buried. Buried, not lost. Not forgotten. Not yet."

Miri traced the edge of the page.

The map she'd found in the satchel was still tucked in her back pocket. She took it out again—still dry, still intact. The circled location was an old bluff just past the edge of the jungle, a place she hadn't walked since childhood.

She remembered following her mother there once, years ago. Rhea had been muttering about patterns in stones. Symbols carved into the cliff walls.

Back then, Miri had rolled her eyes.

Now she rolled the map up and slipped it into her coat.

***

She left the house quietly, avoiding the main road. She wasn't ready to answer questions, to accept condolences from people who'd watched her mother with both reverence and resentment. Varuka had a way of smothering people with silence and calling it respect.

She took the back trail behind the graveyard, past fallen banyan trees and rusted chicken wire. The jungle was thick and dripping from last night's storm. Birds chirped with sharp, warning calls.

The bluff came into view slowly—veiled in mist, perched over a steep drop into jagged rocks. Below, the sea churned.

Miri stepped closer. The air smelled like moss and decay.

Then she saw it.

Carved into the stone near the cliff's edge—barely visible under the growth—was a circle, about a meter wide, surrounded by symbols in old Varukan.

She crouched.

Inside the circle, someone had recently disturbed the earth. Not fully dug, but scraped back. Just enough to know something was hidden here.

She reached for her phone. No signal.

Of course.

She stood slowly.

Then, a sound behind her—small, deliberate. A footstep?

She turned, heart hammering.

But no one was there.

Only the jungle, watching.

Chapter 4

The Council building sat at the centre of the old town square, a low structure of dark stone and shuttered windows. No signs, no symbols. The kind of place that pretended it had nothing to hide—until you tried asking questions.

Detective Naila Deshmukh stood before its doors, listening to the rain patter softly on the awning. Inside, five people waited.

The Elders' Council was not elected. It was inherited. Power passed down through bloodlines disguised as tradition. In theory, they were cultural stewards—keepers of language, history, and ritual. In practice, they were Varuka's shadow government.

Naila stepped inside.

***

The chamber was cool and dark, with a long stone table at its centre. Lamps flickered with oil light.

Incense drifted in the corners, sharp with cinnamon and ash.

She was greeted with nods, not smiles.

Five seats, five faces:

1. Elder Jainu Malel – Silver-haired, slow-moving, always in white. Chairman of the Council. Voice like silk on stone.

2. Elder Navina Aru – The only woman, sharp-eyed, with the soft authority of someone often underestimated.

3. Elder Tambu Deko – Silent, heavyset, hands always folded. Watches everything. Speaks rarely—but always last.

4. Elder Bosha Kaale – Youngest of the five. Smiles too easily. Has contacts off-island. Whispers suggest ambitions.

5. Elder Rafiq Domo – Keeper of oral traditions. A living archive. Refuses to use technology. Considers change a disease.

Jainu gestured toward the centre.

"Detective Deshmukh. You've stirred concern."

"That wasn't my intention," she said evenly.

"You've declared a death suspicious," he continued. "But the physician hasn't confirmed it."

"Because he doesn't have the tools to confirm anything," Naila replied. "But I've seen enough to warrant an investigation."

Rafiq sniffed. "You were not raised here. You don't know the rhythms. Rhea Kaoro was… eccentric. Unwell, some say."

"She had a shell placed in her mouth."

Navina's gaze flicked upward. The others stayed still.

Jainu folded his hands. "And what does that prove?"

Naila stepped forward, voice steady. "It proves someone wanted us to think she died naturally. It proves intention. And if she was researching something dangerous enough to get her killed, we all need to know why."

A long pause followed.

Then, Elder Tambu spoke. Voice slow, thick. "There are truths that belong to the dead."

"And there are crimes that belong to the living," Naila shot back.

No one moved.

Jainu exhaled. "You are permitted to pursue your questions, Detective. But do not mistake curiosity for permission to disrupt. The island has survived by knowing what to forget."

She understood the warning.

As she turned to go, Navina's voice stopped her.

"Detective."

Naila turned.

"If you truly want to know what Rhea Kaoro was chasing," she said, her tone unreadable, "ask about the Eighth Family."

The door shut behind her with a thud that sounded like history slamming shut.

Chapter 5

The soil was loose. Recently disturbed.

Miri crouched beside the stone circle, tracing the faint carvings along its rim. Some were decorative spirals. Others looked like words—old Varukan script, the kind her mother used to sketch in the margins of notebooks.

The ground inside the circle gave slightly beneath her fingers.

She didn't have tools. Just a stick and her hands.

After twenty minutes of careful scraping, her fingers struck something: wood, rotted and soft, barely holding shape. A box, no larger than a shoebox, wrapped in what remained of oilcloth and bark fibre.

She pulled it free.

The lid crumbled.

Inside: scrolls. Water-damaged. Charcoal ink blurred in places. And a fragment of a woven band with eight knots, each tied in a slightly different style.

At the bottom, pressed flat against wood, was a page that had survived the moisture. It bore a name in Varukan.

Her mother had once translated it for her.

"Kama Uvu."

The Forgotten Bloodline.

Her heart clenched.

The Eighth Family.

A name her mother had whispered once in anger. A family that had been struck from the official lineage records, erased from the island's oral and written histories.

A family that wasn't supposed to exist anymore.

She heard something crack in the underbrush behind her and froze—but it was only a lizard skittering across the stone.

Still, she had the sensation she was being watched.

She wrapped the scroll in her jacket and backed away. She'd go back to the house. Study it further. Quietly.

Because if the Eighth Family had been erased…
someone had done the erasing.

And someone might kill to keep it that way.

∗∗∗

Back in her office, Naila spread the old census
logs across her desk.

Six official families were listed in every archive:
names dating back centuries, woven into council seats
and property lines. A seventh—the Kaoro line—had
been added post-colonization, when Varuka
restructured its laws.

But there was a gap.

A blank column where an eighth entry should be.
Not even crossed out—simply gone, like ink removed
with care.

She called the archives. Spoke to an assistant.

"No eighth family on record, Detective. Perhaps
you're misreading—"

"I'm not."

She leaned back in her chair.

The Elders had let the truth fade. Or pushed it.

And Rhea Kaoro had tried to bring it back.

***

That evening, Miri sat cross-legged on the floor of her mother's study, scrolls and torn notes spread out around her.

Naila sat alone in the station's quiet, rain ticking softly against the shutters.

Miles apart, they whispered the same words aloud:

"The Eighth Family was buried."

Neither of them yet knew that what had been buried was more than a name.

It was a crime.

And someone on Varuka was willing to kill again to make sure it stayed that way.

Chapter 7

The graveyard on Varuka's north ridge wasn't marked by headstones, but by weather-worn wood, bundled shells, and small, hand-carved idols pressed into the earth. The official cemetery lay closer to the village, neat and concrete. But this one—the old cemetery—was where the unrecorded were buried.

Naila climbed the hill just before dusk, following rumours.

A witness. A whisperer. A man who "knew the names the Council forgot."

She found him tending a grave with a machete, trimming vines away from a bone-thin marker.

Kelo Tamari looked up when she approached.

"You're walking heavy," he said.

"Gravel's wet."

"I meant with questions."

She hesitated, then handed him a photo of the census page—the gap where a name should be.

"You know what's missing here."

He studied it. Said nothing for a long time.

Then: "A silence like that isn't a mistake. It's a decision."

"You worked as a record keeper once, didn't you? For the old temple?"

"My grandmother did. I listened."

Naila pulled out her notebook. "I need a name. The Eighth Family. The truth."

Kelo wiped his machete on a cloth and gestured for her to follow him.

***

Inside his hut, the walls were lined with books never catalogued by the island archive. Folk stories. Genealogies. Sketches of old prayer markings. On the far wall was a mural—faded charcoal drawings of eight branches twisting from a single trunk.

He pointed to the lowest branch.

"The family was called Uvu. Fishermen. Boat builders. Midwives. They weren't rich, but they had a gift: remembering. Every story, every birth, every death. Oral historians. The Council feared them not because of what they were—but because of what they remembered."

"So, they erased them."

"They couldn't kill all the Uvu," he said softly. "But they made them invisible."

"And Rhea Kaoro found them?"

"She found *evidence*. Proof they existed. Maybe even descendants. That's enough to scare the Council."

Naila's heart picked up. "Do you know who might still carry the name?"

Kelo looked at her for a long time.

Then: "I know who carries the memory. But memory has weight. If you ask them to lift it, you better be strong enough to carry it too."

***

As night fell, he pressed a folded parchment into her hand.

"Find this symbol," he said. "It marks the place where the truth sleeps."

Naila unfolded it.

A symbol with eight interlocking knots—the same motif Miri had found in her mother's scroll.

Chapter 8

Miri spread her mother's notes across the study floor like a ritual.

The house was quiet, save for the ocean wind pressing against the windows. Her mother's scent still lingered—tea leaves, sandalwood, old paper. It made it hard to think. Made it too easy to remember.

A cracked teacup sat on the desk. A smear of ink on a coat sleeve. An unfinished sentence.

"The ones they erased knew everything—too much. They were the island's spine, and that made them dangerous."

Miri ran her finger along the edges of a thin journal marked only with a seashell pressed into wax.

Inside, she found a passage written in hurried script—her mother's voice, fierce and clear:

"The Uvu are not myth. They kept the records before the Council took over. My sources say they preserved the *truth* of what happened during the colonial rebellion. That it wasn't the foreign soldiers who led the massacres—it was Varukans. Our own people. Our own Elders. The Eighth Family tried to reveal it, and for that, they were erased."

Miri sat back hard; breath caught in her throat.

It wasn't just folklore. Her mother had been close to proving it: a massacre whitewashed by official history. And the Eighth Family had been the only ones who dared remember.

No wonder someone wanted the story buried.

She reached for the scroll she'd found near the cliff. Symbols, names, and a faint family tree. Seven branches ended in flames—burned, crossed out, or broken. One remained whole.

A single living line.

A name she didn't recognize—but it had been circled three times in red:

"Natu."

She searched her memories.

That name meant something. She'd heard it— years ago. A woman who came by the house when she was a child. A midwife with gold teeth and hands like weathered bark. She used to bring stories, warnings, sweets wrapped in banana leaves.

Was she still alive?

And if she was… was *she* the last descendant?

Miri tucked the scroll into her bag and stood.

Tomorrow, she'd find the midwife.

And maybe the last living truth of the Eighth Family.

Chapter 9

The morning fog clung low to the island, thick as breath on glass.

Naila stood at the edge of the old harbour, the symbol Kelo had drawn clutched in her hand. Eight knots woven into one another—a design so ancient it no longer appeared in official emblems, and yet... it showed up again and again in Rhea Kaoro's recovered papers.

This time, she'd come to see the one person who might know how symbols like that moved through time: Captain Haru Setele.

***

Haru's ferry had been docked for days, idled by the storm. He sat on the deck repairing a fishing net, smoking cloves. The sea glinted beyond him, deceptively calm.

"You came early," he said without looking up.

"You have a good memory," she replied.

"I remember when people forget things on purpose. What are you forgetting, Detective?"

She handed him the parchment.

He studied it. His fingers paused.

"I've seen this on the hulls of boats," he said. "Old boats. Pre-council days. Symbol of protection."

"And family?"

"Same thing, once."

He pointed to the corner of the parchment, where a faded script curled inward like a tail.

"Most people miss that part."

"What does it say?"

Haru traced the line gently. "It's a funerary tag. A name that shouldn't exist anymore."

Naila's breath caught. "Say it."

"Natu Uvu."

***

She stepped back, heart kicking.

"You're sure?"

"She was a midwife. Worked mostly in the jungle villages. People say she talks to spirits. But I think she remembers the dead better than anyone alive."

"Where is she?"

He gave a sad smile. "If I knew, I wouldn't tell you. But I know where she was seen last. There's a shrine up past the eastern ridge. Carved into stone. That's where the ones who remember go to be alone."

Naila nodded, pocketing the parchment.

"Be careful, Chief," Haru said. "If you ask the past too many questions, it'll start asking back."

***

Miri followed a goat trail through the jungle, the name Natu on her lips like a prayer. She carried only her bag and a photo of her mother. Her footsteps were slow, deliberate.

The jungle opened slightly—revealing a path of worn stones.

And a small shrine carved into the base of a cliff, half-hidden by vines.

Inside sat a woman in a red shawl, hair the colour of ash, skin wrinkled like bark.

She was waiting.

Chapter 10

The Council chamber was dim, as always. But the silence inside felt different now—thicker, more brittle.

The air smelled faintly of damp sandalwood and old stone. Elder Jainu Malel sat at the head of the table, his fingers steepled, eyes closed—not in rest, but calculation.

He was listening. Waiting.

The others were not so patient.

"We should have shut her down at the cliffs," muttered Elder Bosha Kaale, his voice too loud for the space. "The moment she started asking about the shell."

"You want to arrest a police chief?" said Elder Navina Aru, coolly. "That's a good way to set fire to the silence we've spent decades preserving."

"She's not alone now," added Elder Rafiq Domo, who rarely spoke first. "The Kaoro girl is back. She's digging. People talk to her. She looks like her mother."

Jainu finally opened his eyes.

"That's what concerns me most."

***

They had underestimated Rhea Kaoro once—allowed her academic work to continue because it was dismissed as harmless. She was a folklorist, not a revolutionary. A collector of myths.

But now her legacy had become dangerous.

Two investigators.

One sanctioned, the other rogue.

And both following the same trail.

Jainu stood slowly.

"We need to divide the threat," he said. "Naila still believes in institutions. She can be stalled. Redirected."

"And the girl?"

"She's emotional. Personal. Unpredictable."

A pause. Then Elder Tambu Deko spoke, voice like rolling gravel.

"She found Natu."

The room stiffened.

Navina raised an eyebrow. "You're sure?"

"She was seen on the ridge. Someone left offerings after."

Kaale stood abruptly. "We can't let Natu speak."

"She already has," Jainu said. "The question is: what will she say next?"

***

Privately, after the meeting dispersed, Navina remained seated, her gaze fixed on the spiral carvings etched into the table's edge.

She remembered Rhea as a girl—sharp-tongued and too curious. She had admired her once. Maybe still did.

Now she was watching her daughter walk the same path.

She opened the drawer at her side and pulled out a small envelope. Inside: a page torn from one of Rhea's notebooks. Something she had quietly removed from the evidence logs.

The symbol of the Eighth Family.

She traced it gently with her finger.

"The island has a spine," she whispered. "Let's see if it breaks."

Chapter 11

The shrine was little more than a hollow in the cliffside, protected by vines and time.

Inside, Miri sat cross-legged on a woven mat opposite Natu Uvu. The old woman's eyes were clouded but sharp beneath the haze. Her red shawl was wrapped tightly around her shoulders, marked with old embroidery—symbols Miri recognized from her mother's notebooks.

A small oil lamp burned between them.

Outside, the jungle whispered with wind and birdsong. But inside, the silence was sacred.

"You came with your mother's eyes," Natu said at last, her voice cracked but steady.

Miri nodded. "And her questions."

"I warned her once. That some truths don't want to be remembered."

"She remembered anyway."

Natu smiled faintly. "That's what made her dangerous. That's what makes you dangerous now."

Miri leaned forward. "Tell me about the Eighth Family. Tell me what happened."

***

Natu's Testimony

"There were once eight great families on Varuka. Not by blood or wealth—but by trust. Each family held part of the island's memory.

The Uvu were the rememberers. Midwives, death-singers, record-keepers. We knew the names of the drowned and the stories of the born. We didn't write them—we carried them.

When the colonizers came, they tried to erase all of us. But worse than them were the ones who stayed behind after. Our own people. Some of the families… made a deal. They would protect the invaders' power, reshape the island's history—if they were allowed to govern.

And when the Uvu refused to forget, they turned on us. Quietly. Systematically. They erased our names from the census. Burned our homes. Banned our symbols from the temples. Those who lived changed their names. Married into silence.

I was twelve when my mother told me never to speak our name again.

Rhea Kaoro found one of the old birthing songs. It named eight, not seven. That's how she knew. And when she came to me, I told her the rest."

***

Miri listened, stunned. "Why didn't she publish it?"

"She tried. But her publishers wouldn't print it without official corroboration. And the Council blocked it. Quiet pressure. Funding revoked. Archives closed."

"She died because of this, didn't she?"

Natu's eyes dimmed. "She died because someone feared the story would wake."

She reached beneath her shawl and pulled out a worn bundle wrapped in oilcloth. Inside was a carved amulet—the same eight-knot symbol her mother had marked in her journal.

"This belonged to your great-grandmother," Natu said. "Rhea left it with me in case… in case the truth ever found a voice again."

Miri took it, hands trembling.

"You must decide what to do with it," Natu said. "Memory is power. But it's also burden. Are you willing to carry it?"

***

As Miri stepped out into the fading daylight, amulet clenched in her fist, she had her answer.

She wasn't leaving Varuka.

Not until the truth was known.

Even if it killed her too.

Chapter 12

The jungle trail narrowed, flanked by vines as thick as rope and roots that rose like ribs through the mud. Naila moved cautiously, machete in hand, the symbol Kelo had given her etched into her mind.

It had taken her most of the morning to find the path—a goat trail veiled by overgrowth, invisible unless you knew what to look for. But now, in the thick hush of green, she knew she was close.

She stepped into a clearing.

The shrine was exactly as Haru described: a low stone alcove nestled in the cliff's base; its entrance marked by eight carved spirals worn nearly smooth by wind.

She approached, heart quickening.

But the shrine was empty.

No sign of Natu.

No trace of anyone at all—except for a single object left behind:

A folded piece of red cloth.

She knelt beside it. It was still warm.

Someone had been here recently. Maybe moments ago.

She opened the cloth gently.

Inside was a slip of paper, old but intact. In faded charcoal was a name:

"Uvu."

And beneath it, another symbol—one Naila didn't recognize. Not the eight knots. Something newer, scratched in a jagged hand.

It looked like a warning.

***

She stood slowly.

The wind shifted.

Behind her, leaves rustled—too heavy for a bird, too soft for a storm.

She spun; machete raised.

But no one was there.

Only the trees. Watching.

***

Back at the village that evening, Naila stood at the window of her office, staring out at the gathering clouds. The storm hadn't broken yet, but it was circling.

And now she wasn't sure if she was following a truth...

Or walking straight into someone's trap.

She turned back to her desk and drew a line between names.

- Rhea Kaoro
- Natu Uvu
- Miri Kaoro
- Kelo Tamari
- The Eighth Family

The line was starting to form a circle.

And she was standing in the centre.

Chapter 13

The storm finally broke over Varuka like a held breath exhaled all at once.

Sheets of rain lashed the rooftops. Thunder rolled down the cliffs like a drumbeat from the bones of the island. The wind smelled of seaweed and copper and something old.

Naila was halfway back to the station when she saw the figure standing on the road ahead—hood pulled up, soaked to the elbows, arms crossed tight.

Miri.

The look in her eyes was not grief.

It was fury.

***

They took shelter under a crumbling stone overhang once used for drying fish. Rain carved silver rivers down the wall beside them. The silence held for three long breaths.

Then Miri spoke first.

"You found the shrine."

Naila didn't answer.

"You found it, and she was already gone."

Still silence.

Miri stepped closer. "You're chasing shadows. You're filing reports while people are dying for what they remember. My mother—"

"I know who your mother was," Naila cut in. "I was the one who pulled the shell from her mouth. You think I don't care?"

"You didn't know her."

"And you weren't here."

The words landed like a slap.

Miri blinked.

Naila sighed, instantly regretting it. "That was cruel. I'm sorry."

Miri's voice dropped. "But true."

***

For a while, only the rain spoke.

"I found Natu," Miri said finally. "She told me everything. About the Uvu. About what the Council did. About the massacre."

"You believe her?"

"I believe my mother wouldn't die for a lie."

Naila studied her, then nodded. "I've been chasing names. You've been chasing memory. We're on the same path."

"We're not."

"Not yet."

***

Miri pulled something from her pocket—a folded note, rain-damp but legible. The eight-knot symbol. Below it, a name Naila hadn't seen yet.

"Aru."

Naila froze. "That's... one of the Elders."

"Then now we know who to start with."

∗∗∗

Somewhere, a bell rang low. Not a church bell—
a warning bell, struck by hand.

The village was reacting.

Something had happened.

They ran toward the sound together.

For the first time, not as strangers.

Not as rivals.

But as a reckoning.

Chapter 14

The bell was still ringing when Naila and Miri reached the village square.

People were gathered in a loose circle outside the Heritage Archive—the one building meant to preserve Varuka's history. But the double doors hung open now, one of them splintered, the other scorched.

Inside, smoke curled toward the ceiling beams. The fire had been fast, deliberate. The flames were already out—but not before they'd done their work.

Shelves of scrolls had been reduced to ash. Binders left in puddles of melted ink. A scorched map of the island hung on the wall, edges curling like dying leaves.

And in the centre of the room lay a body.

Kelo Tamari.

Face down. Hands burned. A knotwork symbol carved into the wooden floor beside him—eight loops severed at the centre, like a rope violently cut.

Miri fell to her knees.

Naila moved forward, her breath caught halfway to a scream.

There was no blood. No visible wound. But his eyes were open. Wide. As if someone had come not to kill the man—but the memory he carried.

***

That night, the rain never stopped.

The island was hushed, fearful. Doors shut. Lights low. A silence that meant survival.

At the police station, Naila stood before a map pinned to the wall, red threads connecting places, names, dates.

Beside her, Miri cradled Kelo's broken notebook—the one he'd shown Naila days earlier. Half the pages were burned. The rest smelled of smoke and salt.

"He was the last person who remembered freely," Miri whispered. "The Council isn't warning us anymore. They're cleaning house."

"They made a mistake," Naila said.

"Why?"

"They've drawn a line. And they think we're on the wrong side of it."

***

In a locked chamber beneath the Council Hall, Elder Jainu stood with Elder Tambu and Elder Bosha. A small oil lamp burned on the table between them.

"He spoke to both of them," Jainu said, voice low. "He had to be silenced."

"We're running out of shadows," Tambu muttered. "Too many eyes open."

"We still have one card left," Bosha said.

He unrolled a scroll. On it: a list of names. Circled in red—Natu Uvu.

"They want truth? Let them chase it. But they'll never find the whole of it."

"Make sure they don't," Jainu said.

And with that, the order was given.

Chapter 15

By dawn, the storm had softened to a drizzle, but the damage had already spread across Varuka like rot beneath the skin.

Kelo was dead. The archive was gutted. And the island's silence had taken on a new shape—not secrecy, but fear.

Naila and Miri sat across from each other in the station's back room, the map laid out between them, the eight-knot symbol scrawled beside it in fading ink.

"She's next," Miri said.

Naila nodded. "They're going to try to erase her like they did Kelo."

"And if they do—"

"Then the truth dies with her."

***

They moved quickly, quietly.

Naila shed her uniform for plain clothes. Miri packed what was left of her mother's notes and Kelo's journal. Neither of them spoke much as they crossed the village's outer edge, keeping to the coastal paths— avoiding roads, avoiding eyes.

When they reached the ridge trail, the jungle was still damp and steaming. A soft wind rustled the canopy like breath over dry leaves.

"She told me once," Miri said, "that the reason people feared the Uvu wasn't because they remembered too much—but because they never agreed to forget."

Naila glanced sideways. "That's what we're doing now."

***

The shrine came into view through the mist. But this time, Natu wasn't alone.

She was seated beside a small fire. Two other women sat beside her—older, silent, weathered. One braided herb into bundles. The other carved symbols into soft wood.

All three looked up as the women approached.

"You came," Natu said, unsurprised.

"They'll come for you," Miri said, her voice cracking. "We have to get you somewhere safe."

"There's nowhere safe," Natu replied. "But there is still time."

She held up a leather pouch and gestured for them to sit.

"I will tell you everything," she said. "From the beginning. Not the version in your history books. Not the lies whispered into Council chambers. But the story as it was. As it happened. As I remember."

***

For the next hour, she spoke.

Of yet another massacre, this time not led by colonizers but by island leaders who aligned themselves with power.

Of the Eighth Family, blamed, betrayed, and silenced for speaking out.

Of the survivors, scattered into hiding, married under false names, children raised in secret.

And finally, of Rhea Kaoro, who rediscovered the story but didn't know who she truly was until it was too late.

"She wasn't just a scholar," Natu said. "She was a descendant."

Miri froze.

"You mean—?"

"Your mother was Uvu."

Miri's hand flew to the amulet at her neck.

"And so are you."

***

Thunder cracked in the distance.

Naila stood. "We need to move her now."

But Natu held up a hand. "You don't understand. My words are the truth. But they won't be believed until they're heard."

She nodded to a satchel beside her.

Inside: a recording device.

"I've told this story before," she said softly. "To your mother. Now I tell it again. And this time... you'll make sure it lives."

Chapter 16

The jungle was already darker than it should have been.

Rainclouds had returned, thick and low, muffling sound and light. Naila adjusted the weight of her satchel, now heavy with the recorder, notes, and Natu's amulet. Miri moved beside her, one hand gripping Natu's arm, steadying her over the mossy roots.

They were moving fast. Too fast for someone Natu's age.

Behind them, the forest had grown too quiet.

Naila stopped, motioning them to crouch. The rustle of wet leaves behind them wasn't wind.

She unsnapped the blade at her hip.

"Someone's following," she whispered.

Miri's eyes flashed. "How many?"

"Don't know yet. But this isn't random."

Natu, breathing heavily but alert, said, "There's a turn up ahead. A stone path. It leads down to the old salt caves. If they don't know it's there, we can lose them."

Naila nodded.

They ran.

***

They reached the hidden path—a series of moss-slick stones dropping sharply toward the sea cliffs. The cave mouth yawned below like a wound in the earth, barely visible behind hanging vines.

Inside, the salt air stung their nostrils. Ancient storage jars lay smashed in corners, the remnants of a time when the caves held trade goods—and secrets.

"Here," Naila said, pointing to a narrow alcove. "Hide here. Miri, stay with her."

"What about you?"

"I'll draw them off. If they catch us all, it's over."

***

She slipped back up the path, quiet as breath.

And then she saw them—two men in grey tunics, traditional but with modern boots. Moving like hunters. Council agents, not guards. Their eyes were hard. They weren't here to warn anyone.

They were here to erase.

Naila snapped a twig underfoot, intentionally.

One head turned.

She ran.

***

Back in the cave, Miri steadied Natu's hand as she pressed the recorder into hers.

"If they take me," Natu whispered, "you must carry this to the Council. To the people. Don't hide."

"You're not dying here."

Natu gave her a look that was half-smile, half-sorrow. "Then we must move."

***

Naila circled back as rain began to fall again, harder now, drumming the jungle into chaos.

One of the pursuers had followed her too far.

The other… might still be close.

As they regrouped near the water's edge, a faint glow appeared in the trees—a third figure, cloaked and moving carefully.

Naila raised a hand to stop Miri.

"It's not one of them," she whispered.

From the mist stepped Elder Navina Aru.

She looked at them with a mix of resignation and urgency.

And she said:

"If you want this story heard, you'll need more than truth. You'll need *witnesses*. And I'm not the only one ready to speak."

Chapter 17

The cave walls trembled with the sound of distant thunder. But the storm outside wasn't half as dangerous as the one inside the cave.

Naila, Miri, and Natu stood facing Elder Navina Aru, the faint firelight painting her lined face in gold and shadow.

Naila was the first to speak.

"You've been quiet for years."

"I've been waiting," Navina replied, calm as still water.

"For what?"

"For the moment when silence became more dangerous than truth."

***

Miri crossed her arms, body tense. "Why now? After my mother's death? After Kelo?"

Navina didn't flinch. "Because the Council is fractured. Jainu's grip is slipping. Bosha wants control—he'll burn this island to get it. Tambu is old, tired, and will follow whoever feeds his fear."

"And you?" Naila asked. "What do you want?"

"A reckoning," she said. "But not a collapse."

She stepped forward and placed a scroll on the rock between them. "I took this from the archive the night Rhea died. She gave me a copy of her research before the Council moved against her. I buried it, then waited to see if someone would finish what she started."

Naila knelt beside the scroll. It was sealed with Rhea's wax mark—a spiral with eight notches.

"You could've spoken sooner," Miri said.

"I watched my friends disappear for less."

***

Natu, still seated, finally spoke.

"Do you still believe in the Council?"

Navina paused. "No. But I believe the island deserves to heal. We won't get that by tearing it apart overnight. We need evidence. We need allies."

Naila nodded. "Then we go public."

"No," Navina said. "Not yet. If we go public now, Jainu will shut the island down before the next ferry arrives. The broadcast stations are monitored. The post is controlled. We'll need to be strategic."

Miri leaned in. "So, what do you suggest?"

***

Navina looked to each of them in turn.

"There's a ceremonial gathering in two days. Founding Day. The Council speaks before the entire island. It's the only time tradition demands they be silent while others speak."

She pointed to the recorder.

"Play Natu's testimony then. Let the whole island hear what's been buried."

"And if the Council tries to stop us?" Naila asked.

Navina smiled—small, sharp.

"Then we'll know who they really are."

***

As the fire dimmed, and the four women sat beneath the stone ceiling, Naila didn't speak for a while.

She didn't trust Navina—not fully.

But maybe truth needed more than witnesses.

Maybe it needed traitors on the inside.

Chapter 18

The air inside the safehouse was heavy with anticipation. Lanterns flickered low as Naila, Miri, and Navina spread out the map of the village square.

"There's one generator we can tap," Naila said, pointing to a junction near the marketplace. "If we hardwire the speaker system, we can cut the Council's feed and broadcast Natu's recording island-wide."

Miri paced. "And then what? They'll come for us the second it plays."

"Then we give them a choice," Navina said. "Truth… or obedience."

She slid a folded paper across the table.

"These are names of Council members who've expressed doubts. If even one of them breaks ranks publicly after the broadcast—it'll shatter the illusion of unity."

***

On the same night, on the darkened Council Hall, Elder Jainu stared into the flame of an oil lamp.

"We underestimated her daughter," he said flatly.

Elder Bosha prowled like a cornered animal. "It's not just the girl. It's Deshmukh. Aru. The whisperers. Even some of the temple families are murmuring."

Tambu, for once, said nothing. He looked older than ever.

"We shut it down," Bosha snapped. "Founding Day is ceremonial. Cancel it. Declare a day of mourning. Say the weather—"

"No," Jainu interrupted. "If we stop it, we confirm the story is real. We hold the ritual. But we prepare… contingencies."

He pulled out a leather satchel and laid it on the table.

Inside: a small device. Black. Blinking.

Bosha's eyes narrowed. "That's mainland tech. Interference-grade."

"Exactly," Jainu said. "If they try to broadcast…"

"It dies mid-sentence."

Later that night Miri soldered a small transmitter by lantern light, her fingers shaking.

"She died alone, didn't she?" she whispered suddenly.

Naila looked up.

"My mother. She knew they were coming. And I wasn't here. I was painting exhibitions in cities that didn't care if she lived or died."

"She didn't die for nothing," Naila said.

"She might have."

Naila put a hand on her shoulder. "But if we do this right, she won't be the one people remember. They will. The ones who erased her."

***

It was almost midnight. Jainu stood before the sacred fire in the centre of the chamber, hands clasped behind his back.

"We've ruled through silence," he said to no one in particular. "Tomorrow, if they speak… we may have to rule through fear again."

Behind him, the fire cracked.

No one disagreed.

Chapter 19

The sky was still dark, painted in the deep violet just before dawn. The sea was unusually calm—flat like polished stone. Even the birds were quiet.

Inside the safehouse, lit only by a small oil lamp, Miri sat beside Natu, who was wrapped in a thick shawl, her back straight despite her age.

Between them sat the recorder.

A single red light blinked, waiting.

***

"You've heard it all," Natu said. "The truth. The memory. The wound."

Miri nodded. "I still don't know how to carry it."

"You don't carry it alone. That's the lie they made us believe. That we had to."

Miri looked down at the amulet in her palm—eight loops, worn smooth by time. "My mother never told me any of this."

"She wanted to protect you from it," Natu replied. "She thought silence could be safety."

"It wasn't."

"No. But she tried. That's what mothers do. Even when they fail."

Miri's voice broke slightly. "I hated her for not asking me to stay."

"And she hated herself for not asking you louder."

***

A long silence passed.

Then Natu reached for the recorder and pressed *play*.

Her voice filled the room—clear, unwavering.

"This is the account of the massacre not written in your books. This is the name of the family that remembered when others chose to forget…"

Miri listened as the voice that once spoke only in whispers became evidence.

She wiped a tear from her cheek and looked to the window.

Light was beginning to edge over the sea.

***

Natu looked at her.

"They will try to shout us down."

"I'll shout louder."

"They may come for you next."

"I'm my mother's daughter."

***

And then, as the sun began to rise over Varuka, Miri stood, tucking the recorder into her jacket.

"Let's end the forgetting."

Chapter 20

The square was packed.

Beneath the fluttering white banners of Founding Day, villagers filled every step, every stall, every shadowed alley. Children wore woven sashes, elders carried palm fronds, and the drums of the north quarter played their slow ancestral rhythm.

On the surface, it looked like every year before.

But the crowd was too quiet.

Eyes scanned rooftops.

Voices murmured instead of cheered.

And near the central stage, Council guards stood closer together than usual, hands resting too comfortably near weapons they were not supposed to carry during ceremony.

***

Naila stood beneath the platform scaffolding, dressed in civilian clothes, her badge tucked away. Her eyes swept the square, noting the speaker towers, the rigged junction box, the wire she'd threaded behind the vendor stall.

All still intact.

But her gut twisted.

Something was wrong.

***

Miri, seated in the front row with the satchel on her lap, didn't blink.

She'd pressed the amulet flat beneath her palm.

She couldn't see Natu, who waited two blocks away with Navina and three others in a small, hidden van. But she felt her presence like a thread running taut through her chest.

The recorder was warm against her ribs.

***

On stage, Elder Jainu approached the podium.

His white robes were spotless. His face unreadable.

He placed both hands on the carved wooden surface and said, with soft solemnity:

"We gather again beneath the spirit of remembrance…"

***

In a hidden alcove behind the Council Hall, Elder Bosha moved quickly.

He carried the interference device—small, sharp-edged, blinking red. It was designed to fry the signal the moment it activated. It had worked before, quietly, invisibly.

But this time…

He hesitated.

Someone had tampered with the wiring.

***

Back in the crowd, Naila saw the guard move. Subtle. A signal passed by eye contact.

She turned toward the stage.

Too early.

They were planning something.

***

Jainu's speech droned on. Tradition. Prosperity. Peace.

The old script.

But Naila saw his fingers twitch against the wood.

He was waiting for something too.

***

Then, a sharp snap of feedback crackled through the speakers—just for a moment.

The crowd stirred.

Jainu paused. Only for half a second. Then continued.

But Naila moved.

She slipped behind the stage, toward the equipment tent.

The signal was being jammed.

The sabotage was real.

***

At the same time, Miri rose from her chair.

She didn't wait for Naila's sign.

She walked to the platform steps, recorder in hand, and climbed.

Gasps followed her.

One of the guards reached out to stop her—

—and then froze, because Navina Aru stepped into view from the opposite side, in full ceremonial robes, and nodded once.

It was time.

Chapter 21

The recorder sat on the podium like a quiet threat.

Miri's hand hovered over the play button, her mouth dry, her heart beating like a war drum in her chest. The village square was silent, breath held, eyes locked.

Somewhere deep in the crowd, a child whispered: *"That's the daughter."*

On the stage behind her, Elder Jainu stood stiff, his expression carved from stone.

From the edge of the square, Navina Aru held the gaze of the other Elders—daring them to speak. Daring them to break the ritual silence of Founding Day.

But below the stage, in the equipment tent, the real threat had already begun.

***

Naila crouched behind the junction box, tools in hand, eyes scanning wires.

The signal light had flickered twice.

Someone had tampered with the backup line.

Cut the feed now, and the broadcast dies before it ever begins.

She followed the cable trail to the generator—a small steel box humming behind crates of ceremonial flowers.

And there—a figure crouched in the shadows.

Black gloves. Grease-stained shirt. A Council agent, rewiring the relay.

Too fast for sabotage.

Too slow for subtlety.

Naila didn't wait.

She lunged.

***

The two collided hard against the generator. The man snarled, grabbing at the cable, trying to yank it free.

Naila drove her elbow into his side, twisting the pliers from his grip. He recovered, reached for a hidden blade— and she pulled her badge out of her pocket and slammed it into his temple.

He dropped.

But the relay sparked.

The signal light turned red.

The speakers flickered.

***

On stage, Miri's finger was on the play button.

She glanced at Naila—who now stumbled into view, blood on her arm, mouth open, shouting—

"NOW! PLAY IT!"

***

Miri hit play.

***

A crackle surged through the speakers.

The crowd flinched.

And then: Natu's voice.

"This is the account of what was buried…"

The Council didn't move.

Not yet.

But behind their blank stares, something was breaking.

And in the square, the people listened—really listened—for the first time in generations.

Chapter 22

"This is the account of what was buried."

Natu's voice—clear, unbroken—rang through the square, carried across old speakers that crackled but held.

"My name is Natu Uvu. I am the last born of the Eighth Family. We were the keepers of memory. We remembered births, deaths, and the moments in between. That is why they came for us."

The crowd stood frozen.

Some gasped. Some wept. Others simply stared.

Children clutched their parents' hands. Elders whispered names they hadn't spoken in years.

"They told you it was the colonizers who burned the salt villages. But it was not. It was our own. The island leaders aligned themselves with outside power—and to secure their place, they gave up ours."

On the stage, Elder Jainu's jaw tightened, but he did not move.

"We were marked. Our names scratched out of temple scrolls. Our symbols forbidden. The knot of eight—our family crest—was declared dangerous. A superstition. We became ghosts in our own land."

Miri's hand shook.

But she did not stop the recording.

***

In the crowd, voices rose.

"She's telling the truth."

"I've seen that knot. My grandmother had it sewn into her shawl."

"They said it was a protection charm."

"It was a name."

***

"Rhea Kaoro found our name again. She asked the questions others feared. She found the story in a lullaby, hidden

in the tongue of the old women, passed hand to hand like a hot coal. And for that, they silenced her."

Gasps rippled through the crowd.

Naila saw one Council guard step back, shaken.

"The Elders who did this may be dead. But the ones who protect their lies are not."

"You know them."

"You've sat before them."

"And now you must choose."

***

The recording ended.

For one full second, the silence was total.

Then a voice rose—small, but firm:

"She's right."

Another joined it: "We remember the Kaoro woman. She came to our village. She asked. She listened."

Then a shout: "Why did you lie to us?!"

All eyes turned to the Council platform.

And for the first time in decades, the Elders did not speak.

Because there was nothing left to say.

Chapter 23

They didn't run.

That was the first surprise.

As the crowd surged with questions, accusations, and awakening, the Council Elders remained on the platform—stoic, unflinching.

But their stillness was not unity.

It was paralysis.

Jainu raised his hand—not to silence, but to steady.

"People of Varuka," he began, voice tight, formal. "You have heard stories. From beyond our halls. Stories twisted with grief. With personal agendas. We mourn Rhea Kaoro. But we must not mistake sorrow for fact—"

"Enough."

The word came from behind him.

The crowd gasped.

Elder Tambu Deko—silent for years, obedient for decades—stepped forward.

"Enough lies," he said again.

Jainu turned, thunderstruck.

Tambu's voice was gravel, but it carried. "I was there. Not on the night of fire. But in the years after. I signed the orders to strike the Uvu name from the temple register. I knew what I was doing. We all did."

A silence louder than the crowd followed.

"I'm tired of pretending truth is dangerous," Tambu said. "We are the danger. Not the stories."

***

Bosha stepped forward, face red. "This is madness."

"It's memory," Tambu said. "And it's time we faced it."

He stepped down from the platform and stood among the crowd.

And then others followed.

First a teacher. Then a merchant. Then a retired priest who had been quiet for years. One by one, voices broke the long silence.

***

Backstage, Naila and Miri watched from the edge of the scaffolding.

"They're splitting," Naila said quietly.

"Do you think it's real?"

"I think the story's too big to bury now."

Miri didn't answer.

She was watching Jainu, whose face was composed but whose knuckles were white on the edge of the platform.

He hadn't lost. Not yet.

But he'd been seen.

Chapter 24

Night had fallen again.

The Council Hall sat heavy with shadows, lit only by the central flame. A few loyal guards remained outside, but the people no longer looked to them with reverence. Only suspicion.

Inside, Elder Jainu Malel stood at the centre of the chamber, pacing slowly.

"They will remember this," he said aloud.

But no one answered.

Only Bosha stood nearby, arms crossed, seething. Tambu was gone. Navina, vanished into the crowd. Rafiq had not spoken since the broadcast.

"We built this," Jainu said. "We gave them peace. Identity. Order."

Bosha spat on the floor. "You gave them a lie, old man. And now they know how to listen."

***

Outside, the square had not emptied. People lit candles. Stories were being shared aloud, like embers passed from hand to hand. The eight-knot symbol—once a forgotten sigil—was now sketched into dust, etched into fabric, worn openly.

Miri and Naila stood near the centre, watching as the people reclaimed memory, together.

Then Naila's radio crackled.

"Signal detected—broadcast signal, Council line—standby..."

***

Back in the Hall, Jainu placed a small device on the central table. An override module, used during coastal emergencies to seize island-wide comms.

He activated it.

His voice cut into every speaker in the square.

"People of Varuka," he began, voice iron-clad. "You are being misled. A single recording does not rewrite history. Do not fall to emotion. Return to your

homes. Do not let disorder poison what we've built—
"

But then the sound warped. Cracked. Stopped.

***

In the crowd, people looked up.
Static. Then silence.

***

Naila spoke softly into her mic.
"He didn't know we redirected the broadcast lines."
Miri looked at her. "We burned his last script."

***

In the Council Hall, Jainu stared at the now-dead mic.
Behind him, two guards lowered their eyes.

The door creaked open.

Navina entered. Alone.

She said nothing. Just stood there.

Waiting.

***

The next morning, the Council Hall was empty.

The doors left open.

The people came not to protest, but to witness.

Because the silence, at last, belonged to them.

Chapter 25

The sun broke over Varuka for the first time in what felt like days—clear, golden, quiet. The square had emptied. The banners had been taken down. But change still hummed in the stones.

Inside the police station, Naila flipped through a final report. Her desk was stacked with statements, recordings, testimonies.

Everything pointed to the Council's rot.

But only one name was linked directly to the night Rhea Kaoro died.

A quiet knock at the door.

Miri entered, holding a weathered envelope.

"She gave me this," she said, laying it down. "Natu. Said my mother left it with her in case... things went wrong."

Naila opened it carefully.

Inside: a journal page. Rhea's handwriting.

"If they find this, it means I was right. It won't be the Council who kills me—it will be the one who watches quietly.

The one who smiled through my questions. The one who once called me 'friend.'"

At the bottom: a single name.

Elder Bosha Kaale.

***

Miri stared at it.

"I thought it was Jainu."

"He gave the orders," Naila said. "But Bosha was the one who acted. He was the Council's blade."

***

Flashback (briefly interwoven as a memory, from Rhea's notes and Naila's investigation):

He came to her home after dusk, under the guise of sharing new archive access. He waited until she turned her back. He placed the shell himself—knowing the symbolism. Knowing it would sow confusion.

He made it look like a suicide.

He walked out without a mark on him.

***

Back in the present:

"He's gone," Naila said. "Disappeared after the broadcast. The harbour master said someone left on a skiff the night before the Council dissolved. No name. Just cash."

Miri was silent for a moment. Then:

"Then he gets to vanish?"

"No." Naila stood. "He gets to be remembered."

***

She reached for the radio mic.

"Dispatch to port control. Be advised: we're issuing a warrant. Bosha Kaale. Suspected in the murder of Rhea Kaoro. And wanted for obstruction of truth."

She paused.

"International alert. Do not let the sea carry him away."

Chapter 26

Three weeks later, the sea was gentle.

Children played again along the harbour. Vendors reopened their stalls. And the shrine at the western cliffs—once hidden, half-buried—now had candles burning outside it every night.

Someone had carved the eight-knot symbol into the stone above its entrance.

The people didn't call it the Eighth Family shrine anymore.

They called it the Place of Remembering.

***

Inside the newly reopened Heritage House, Miri stood among workers carefully restoring books, scrolls, and fragments saved from the archive fire. The ceiling had been patched. The walls repainted. But the soul of the place was now something entirely new.

"I still don't know how to run a cultural centre," she said, holding a cracked teacup from her mother's old office.

Naila leaned against the doorframe. "You've got half the island donating their grandparents' memories. That's how it starts."

Miri smiled. "I keep waiting for the grief to turn off."

"It doesn't. It just... changes shape."

She nodded. "What about you?"

"I've been asked to stay," Naila said. "Full term. Head of a new civilian-led oversight body. Separate from the old Council."

Miri raised an eyebrow. "So, you're going to stay?"

"I think this island still needs watching. But maybe not in the way it used to."

***

They walked to the front steps together, where candles burned in a line along the road.

A group of children knelt beside the pathway, painting symbols on smooth stones—spirals, waves, stars. And eight-knots.

"They're rewriting the island," Miri said.

"No," Naila said. "They're finally writing it down."

***

In the distance, a boat arrived from the mainland—full of visitors, scholars, perhaps sceptics. But no one on the island looked afraid anymore.

Not of truth.

Not of remembering.

Chapter 27

The grave was simple.

A flat stone set beneath the flowering tamarind tree Rhea had planted when Miri was born. Around it grew wild thyme and drifting petals from the nearby shrine. On the stone, carved by local hands:

Rhea Kaoro

Mother. Rememberer. Unbroken.

Miri knelt, brushing windblown blossoms from the inscription.

She didn't speak at first. Just listened—to the breeze, the sea, the voices of children playing farther down the path. The island was no longer quiet in fear. It was alive in memory.

"I should have come back sooner," she whispered.

"But I came back. And I stayed."

She placed a stone atop the grave. Painted on it: the eight-knot symbol.

***

Behind her, footsteps.

Naila approached slowly, carrying two paper cups of coffee. She passed one to Miri without speaking.

Together, they stood in silence for a moment—until Miri finally said:

"I think I'm ready to call this home again."

Naila smiled. "Good. The island has enough ghosts. It needs more witnesses."

They sat on the stone wall together, overlooking the valley where new gatherings were forming. Oral history circles. Music from forgotten scales. Children repeating rhymes their grandparents once feared to say aloud.

"You know," Miri said, sipping, "we make a decent team."

"Don't tell anyone," Naila said. "I've got a reputation for being difficult."

"You're impossible."

"And yet," Naila added, "we cracked the silence."

***

Miri reached into her satchel and pulled out a new notebook—blank, leather-bound.

She opened it to the first page and wrote, in her mother's language:

"For those who were erased. For those who remembered. And for those who dared to listen."

She looked up at Naila.

"Ready to start the next story?"

Naila raised her cup in a quiet toast.

"Always."